My Tiny Pet

Jessie Hartland

Nancy Paulsen Books

NANCY PAULSEN BOOKS
an imprint of Penguin Random House LLC, New York

Visit us online at penguinrandomhouse.com

SEP 0 3 2019

Library of Congress Cataloging-in-Publication Data
Names: Hartland, Jessie, author.
Title: My tiny pet / Jessie Hartland.
Description: New York, NY: Nancy Paulsen Books, [2019]
Summary: After moving to a tiny house, a little girl is forbidden to get a pet until she introduces her parents to microscopic tardigrades, also called water bears.
Identifiers: LCCN 2018044997 | ISBN 9781524737535 (hardcover: alk. paper) | ISBN 9781524737566 (ebook) | ISBN 9781524737542 (ebook)
Subjects: | CYAC: Family life—Fiction. | Small houses—Fiction. | Pets—Fiction. | Tardigrada—Fiction.
Classification: LCC PZ7.H2638 My 2019 | DDC [E]—dc23
LC record available at https://lccn.loc.gov/2018044997

Manufactured in China by RR Donnelley Asia Printing Solutions Ltd.
ISBN 9781524737535
10 9 8 7 6 5 4 3 2 1

Design by Dave Kopka. Text set in Pacella ITC Std. The art is painted in gouache.

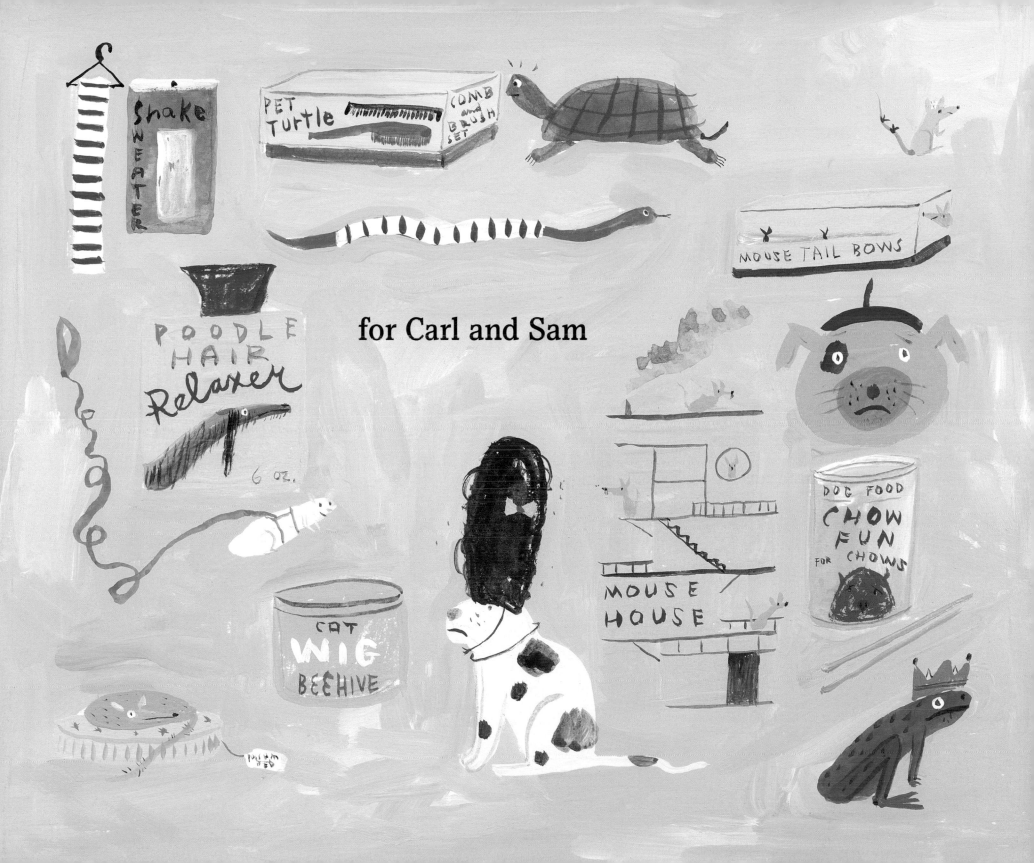

for Carl and Sam

Once upon a time,
not so very long ago,
I lived in a ginormous
house on a tall hill in
a big, noisy town.

We had six poodles,
ten cats, a tarantula, two
snakes, three hedgehogs,
ten mice, countless birds,
several saltwater tanks with
hundreds of fish,

an octopus,
three rabbits,
a pony, a pig, a goat
and a trio
of turtles.

A few pets later,
Mom walked in
the door and said,

"Simplify!"

And Dad said,

"Downsize!"

I was sad.
But all the pets
went to good
homes.

Now we live in
a tiny house.

We like the simple life
in the woods:

Time to read.

Time to draw.

Time to daydream.

Then I learn something exciting in
science that gives me an idea.

So I bring up the pet subject *again* at dinner.

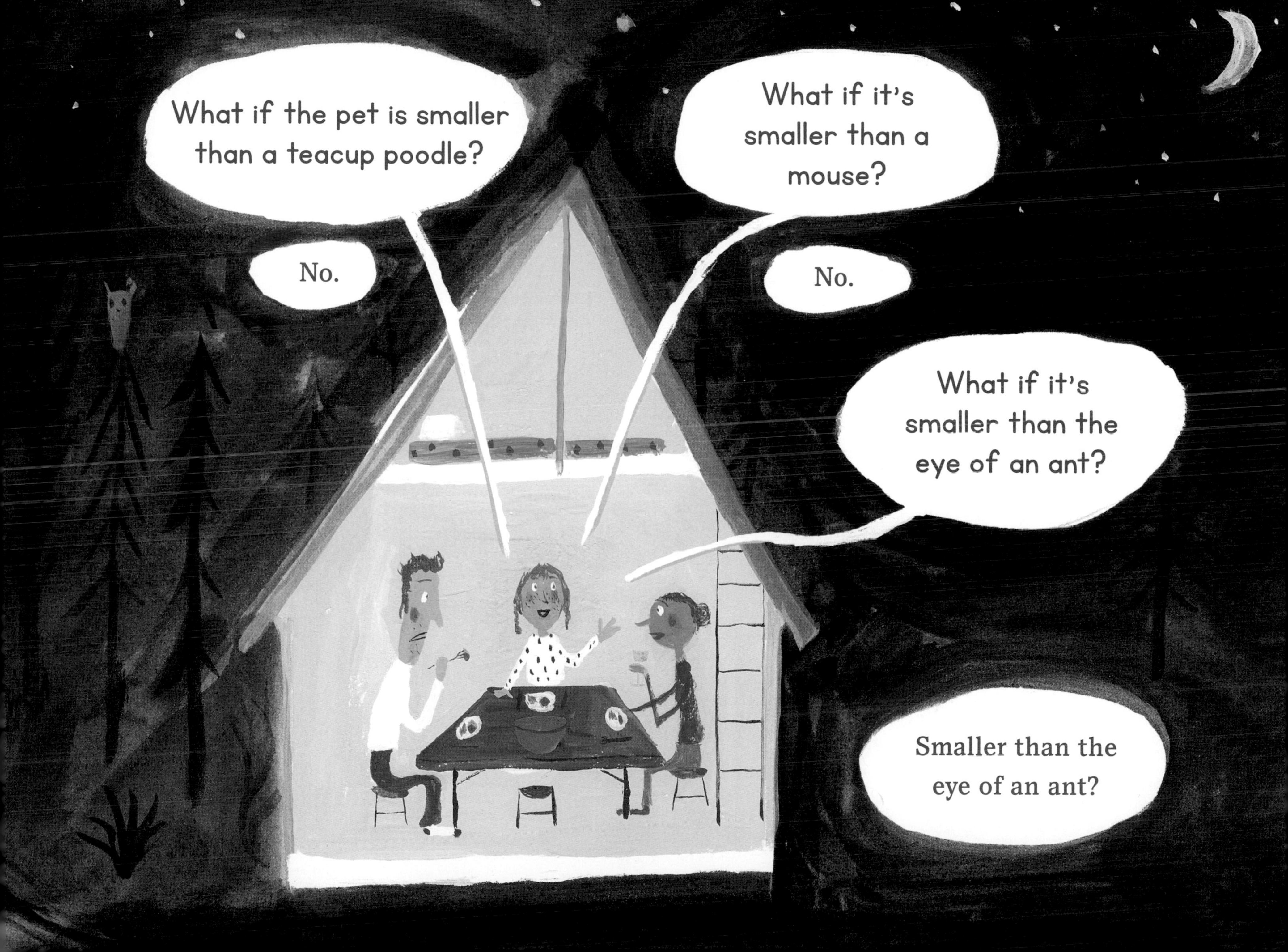

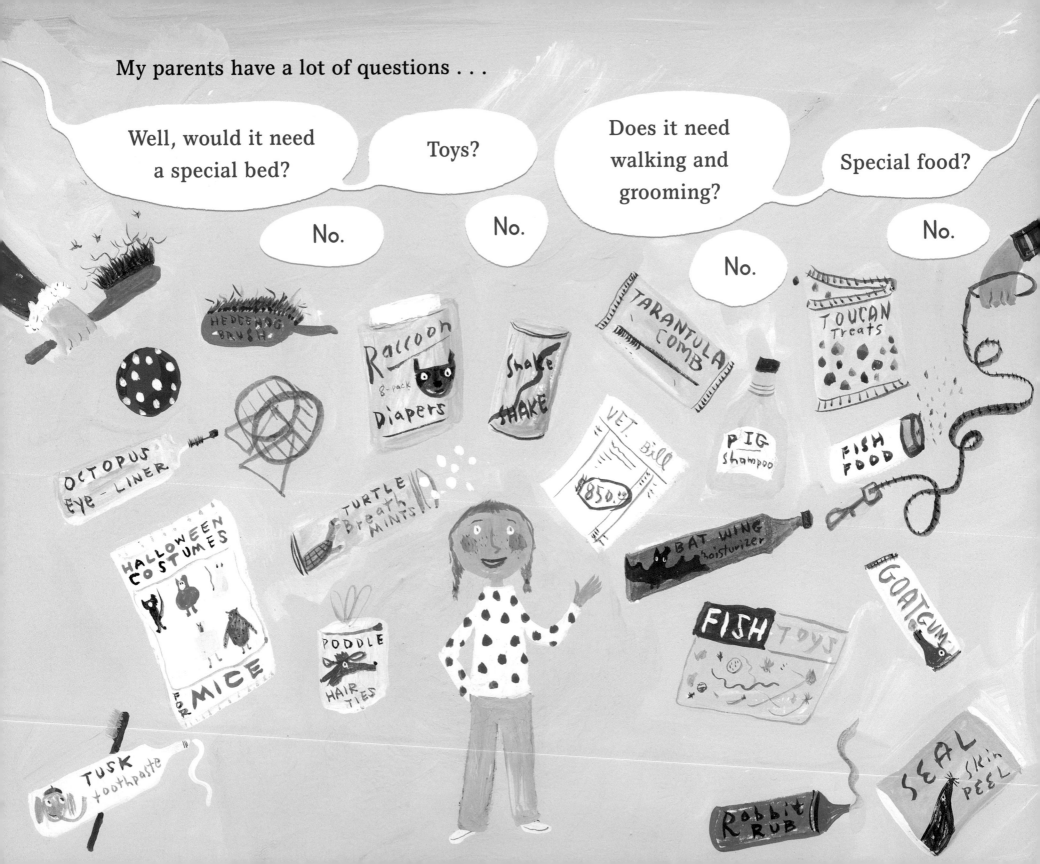

I don't mention that I'll need a microscope to look at it.

The next day, I take my parents for a walk in the woods and tell them, "You find these animals living in moss."

"What is it?"

"It's a kind of bear," I tell them.

"A bear?"

"Bears are BIG."

"Not this bear," I said.
"This bear is tiny."

"Really? That's it?"
my parents ask.

"Now, THAT is small."

At home, I show it to them
magnified 300 times.

"It's perfect," I tell them.

But they still have
another question . . .
"How BIG does it get?"

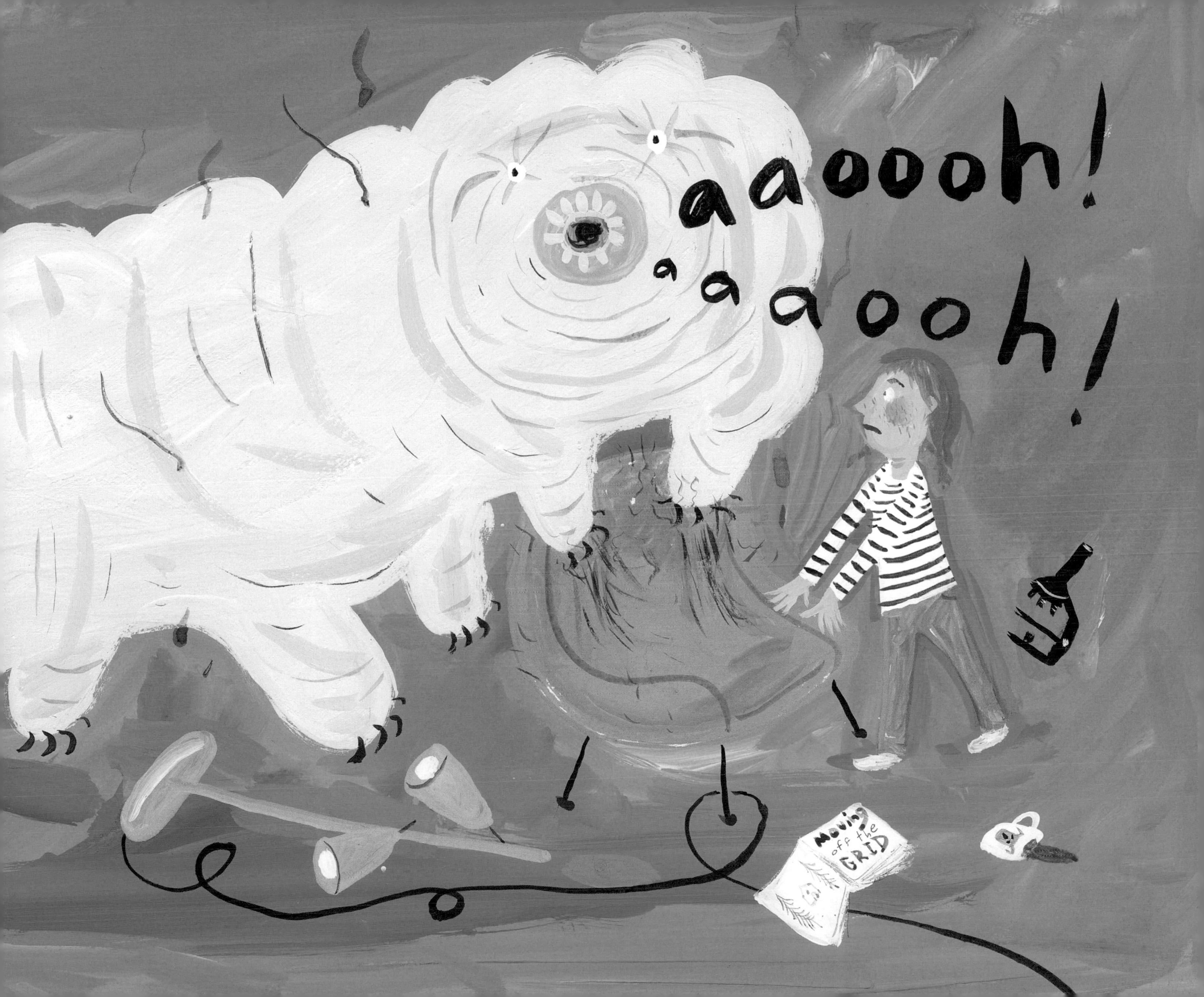
aaoooh!
aaaooh!
MOVING off the GRID

And having a tiny pet
has so many advantages!

I can take my
water bear
with me
wherever
I go.

I take it here. I take it there.
I take it anywhere.

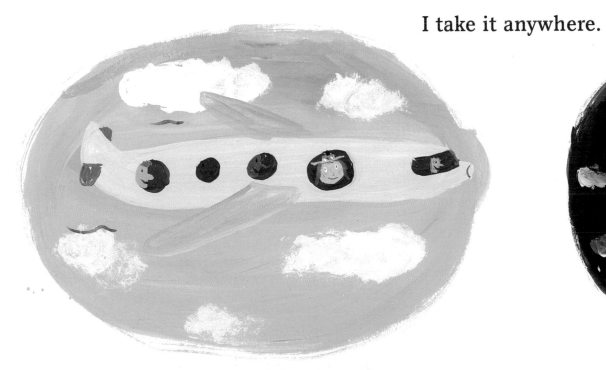

So everything is great—until one day,
I hear something familiar . . .

Dad says, **"Simplify!"**

And Mom says, **"Downsize!"**

But it's OK!
I know that no
matter how small
we go . . .

. . . there will
always be room
for my tiny pet.

Author's Note

With the tiny house movement—and downsizing—gaining popularity, I had the idea for a story about a tiny pet in a tiny house. I thought back to my favorite science class, protozoology, and my choice specimen, the lively single-celled paramecium. But then I remembered the *Life at the Limits* show at New York's American Museum of Natural History and its eye-catching subway posters featuring a tardigrade, and I knew I had my story's perfect pet. This extremely resilient animal can live just about anywhere in the world, from the highest mountains to the deepest seas, and is certainly tiny, usually less than five-hundredths of an inch long.

Eye of Science/Science Source

These microscopic animals have been around for more than 600 million years but were first described in the 1770s by zoologist Johann Goeze as *kleiner Wasserbär*, German for "little water bear." A few years later, Italian naturalist Lazzaro Spallanzani dubbed them *tardigrada*, or "slow steppers."

A few more fun facts about the tardigrade:

- They are the first known animal to survive in outer space.

- They can swim in boiling water.

- They shrivel into a blob when life conditions become threatening, but can later come alive again! This is called *cryptobiosis*.